MW00873787

Imagine a mommy, and what you'd expect.

One day super human. Another? A wreck.

Invisible labor? Check, check, & checked!

It's not nature or nurture; it's not her birthright.

Yet it grows more every day—nearly a blight.

So many frustrated mommies, in a mask that's polite.

The mommy in our story falls into the norm.

She's loving and kind, affectionate and warm.

Perhaps a bit frazzled—but knows how to perform.

So what's the big deal? Why all the noise?

We're so glad you asked! Listen up, girls & boys.

And we'll tell you how mommy creates a life she enjoys.

Most days it starts with an alarm and a groan.

With so much to get done, and no way to postpone.

She yearns for a snuggle, a book, & a scone.

But there's breakfast, backpacks, and a spilled milk scare.

The meticulous brushing of tangle-y hair.

And the occasional cry of, "But that's so unfair!"

It's the steak she always forgets to defrost.

And the pile of laundry to be sorted and washed.

Then put right away—except that one sock that's lost.

There's the longing to take a quick nap after lunch.

But the deadline is looming, and time's in a crunch.

Plus there's talk of promotion, and she's got a hunch.

It's two full-time jobs, which take up the whole day.

Crushing at work, then scouts and ballet.

So it's key that mommy also makes time to play.

When the kids are asleep and her brain slows its spin,

Mommy rolls up a joint and takes that shit in.

Her fav is the Kush, 'cause it widens her grin.

What is this "Kush", you may want to know?

Why, it's cannabis! It's a plant you can grow.

(Well… only in places that are truly down, though.)

It's sticky, and dank, and a luscious bright green.

It softens sharp edges, so life takes on a sheen.

And helps ease the stress of the unforeseen.

But wait… there's more! We have only begun.

The effects are miraculous, second to none.

Many folks love it, although not everyone.

# Latest Chronicle

## 62% AMERICANS SUPPORT CANNABIS LEGALIZATION

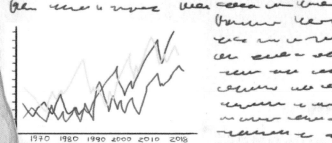

But for those who partake, it does a whole lot.

Stress, anxiety, pain? What've *you* got?

This plant is a miracle; I kid you not.

Our mommy, for instance, who rarely waits for night.

She could struggle all day, or reach for a light.

And puff on her kind bud to set things back right.

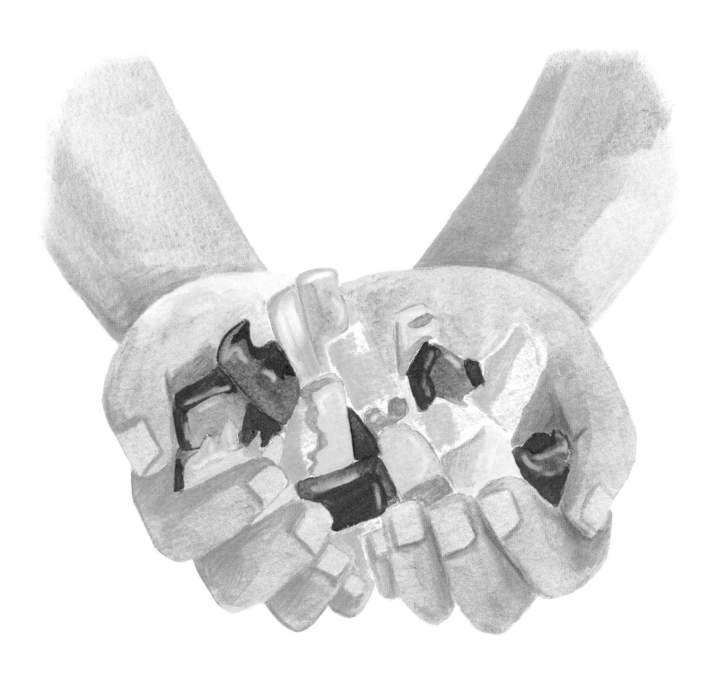

She might also nibble a sweet little gummy.

And ride the fun buzz as it melts in her tummy.

Mommy knows the right dosage; she ain't no dummy.

She adores her vape pen, as it's super discreet.

It's tiny and quiet, the smell nice and sweet.

A few puffs and she's good—a workday retreat.

Daddy also enjoys a few tokes a day.

And smoking together helps their sex life—hurray!

They puff on a nug and then take time to play.

Then we've got the medicine of pure CBD.

It's great for sore shoulders, elbows, or knees.

Aunty loves a few drops in her glass of Chablis.

Adults everywhere are enjoying this high.

Don't matter if it's Afghani, Cali, or Thai.

Those stresses & worries can all go bye-bye.

Mommy especially loves to smoke a big bowl.

The fresh, skunky flower helps to reboot her soul...

And reminds her that joy is her favorite goal.

So no more frantically searching for the sock.

Instead she tosses its twin & goes for a walk.

Or simply kicks back, looks around, and takes stock.

Or puts off the dusting, the laundry, and dishes.

(And all other chores which are repetitious.)

To focus on the joyful, fun, and delicious.

When it comes to the kids, a buzz sure makes things fun!

Mommy crawls in the grass, and plays in the sun.

She's not scared to be silly, unleashed, or undone.

No need to stress out about what is for dinner.

Or compare to friends who are richer or thinner.

Instead listen to that which is subtle and inner.

It says to be open to children's perspective.

To honor uniqueness, and outlooks subjective.

To not push agendas or be too directive.

It encourages authentic and heart-felt connection.

To chill in a moment of peaceful reflection.

That there's no such thing as human perfection.

So is mommy happier when she puffs on the kind?

You be the judge, but keep one thing in mind:

This plant changes lives, if you are so inclined.

## About the Author

A loving partner and stepmom living in a state with legal recreational cannabis, the author is well acquainted with the benefits of this beautiful plant. She advocates for the normalization of cannabis, and hopes that this book will open conversations between users and non-users alike.
You can reach her at elizagreenflower@gmail.com

Made in the USA
Monee, IL
06 July 2021

73058133R00036